The Adventures of
The Gingerbread Man

Also in Beaver by Elizabeth Walker

The Gingerbread Man in Winter

The Adventures of The Gingerbread Man

Elizabeth Walker

Illustrated by Lesley Smith

Beaver Books

A Beaver Book
Published by Arrow Books Limited
62-65 Chandos Place, London WC2N 4NW

An imprint of Century Hutchinson Limited

London Melbourne Sydney Auckland
Johannesburg and agencies throughout
the world

First published by Hutchinson Children's Books in 1986
Beaver edition for Ashton Scholastic, Australia 1986
Beaver edition 1987
Reprinted 1989

Text © Elizabeth Walker 1986
Illustrations © Lesley Smith 1986

Set in Baskerville
by Book Ens, Saffron Walden, Essex

Printed and bound in Great Britain by
The Guernsey Press Co Ltd
Guernsey, C.I.

ISBN 0 09 949660 7

Contents

The Gingerbread Man

A little old woman began to bake
And at once she knew what she'd like to
  make,
'I'll mix him and pat him and find him a pan,
And then I shall have me a gingerbread man.'

But soon from the oven there came forth a
  squeak,
That gingerbread man had decided to speak.
'Let me out, let me out,' he cried out with
  glee –
When she opened the oven he shouted, 'I'm
  free!'

He dashed to the door, he raced through the
  gate,
That gingerbread man shouted out, 'I'll not
  wait!
I'll jump and I'll run till I've seen all this
  place.'
And away on adventures the little man raced.

And that gingerbread man is still with us
today,
You've only to ask him to come out and play.
But how will you find him? Just see if you
can –
You make him and bake him – a gingerbread
man!

1

The Gingerbread Man
And The Rain

Once upon a time there was a little gingerbread man. He had been made by a little old woman in a little house by a wood, and he was only one day old. He was crisp and brown, and his currant eyes were sharp as buttons, and he ran through the fields very proudly.

'I'm a gingerbread man, just look and see,
There's no one in the world as clever as me,
I run so fast, I jump so high,
Quite soon I'll even touch the sky!'

So sang the little gingerbread man, running through the tussocky grass and leaping over dandelions.

A snail sitting on a leaf slowly lifted its strange spiky head and said 'If I were you little man I'd shout a little less loudly.'

The gingerbread man stopped. 'What a strange thing you are,' he said. 'How lucky I am to be a gingerbread man and not ugly and slimy like you. I shall shout just as loud as I like.'

And off he ran, bounding over the ground

while the snail shook his head and said slowly, 'You'll learn, little man, you'll learn.'

On went the gingerbread man, through a hedge, under a fence, always singing his song.

'I'm a gingerbread man, just look and see,
There's no one in the world as clever as me,
I run so fast, I jump so high,
Quite soon I'll even touch the sky!'

A butterfly perched on the branch of an apple tree, fluttered her bright wings and whispered in a voice like silver bells, 'Oh little man, don't shout so loud. Someone will hear you.'

'What do I care?' said the gingerbread man proudly. 'Only this morning I was baked, and since then I have run and jumped and shouted. I'm not weak and fluttery like you, and I can shout as loud as I like. For I am made out of gingerbread!' And to prove how strong he was, the gingerbread man bounced right up to the apple tree branch and down again to the ground, bounce, bounce!

The butterfly shook her lovely head. 'You'll learn little man, you'll learn,' she said. 'Hide now, for the rain is coming.'

But the little gingerbread man didn't know about rain, for he'd only been baked that very day. So he laughed and shouted once again:

'I'm a gingerbread man, just look and see,
There's no one in the world as clever as me,
I run so fast, I jump so high,
Quite soon I'll even touch the sky.'

And he leaped up as high as ever he could. But he didn't touch the sky. He didn't even get right to the top of the apple tree.

And in the sky, that was many times higher than the gingerbread man could jump, great grey clouds were gathering. The rain had heard the gingerbread man and was about to teach him a lesson.

'Hide, little gingerbread man,' whispered the butterfly, and with a flutter of wings she flew away to shelter in the hedge. The gingerbread man laughed and sniffed the apple blossom.

Just then a large drop of rain plopped down next to him. The gingerbread man was puzzled. 'What is this?' he said. 'Wherever did you come from?'

But the raindrop said nothing at all. Another fell with a splash on the other side of the ginger-bread man and a little went on to his leg.

'Oh!' cried the gingerbread man. 'You are very cold and wet. Go away! I said, go away!'

But of course the raindrop stayed just where it was, except that it spread a little and some more went on to the gingerbread man's leg. And a little of his mixture began to go soggy.

'Stop it! Stop it I say!' cried the gingerbread man. 'You are spoiling me!'

But instead of stopping the rain began to fall harder, and in the distance came the low rumble of thunder.

The little gingerbread man felt very frightened. He crept as far under a leaf as he could, and pulled his arms and his legs tightly round him, but even so he could feel his edges going soggy in the rain. A little piece of his foot crumbled right away.

'Oh dear, oh dear!' he cried 'I see that I should not have shouted so loudly. Soon I shall become so wet that there will be nothing left of me at all and I was only baked this morning!' And one of his sugar buttons fell with a plop on to the ground.

High in the sky the clouds and the rain heard the little gingerbread man and the thunder rumbled in his big voice, 'He's not a bad fellow. Only a little silly.'

And the raindrops pattering down whispered in their little voices, 'Yes, yes, he is a foolish little gingerbread man.'

So the wind blew from the west and soon the clouds were swept from the sky and the sun was shining.

The little gingerbread man looked out from

under his leaf. He picked up his lost button and put it back on his jacket, then he gathered up his crumbling foot and patted it back into shape. The warmth of the sun made him crisp and strong again.

'Perhaps I am not so clever after all,' he said. 'I must think of a new song to sing.'

And away he went, bounding over the

dandelions and the tussocky grass. But this time he sang:

'I'm a gingerbread man, it's me again,
I nearly got drowned in some very wet rain,
But now I am crisp and strong as can be,
So thank you dear sun for your kindness to
    me.'

But this was only the start of the gingerbread man's adventures.

2

The Gingerbread Man and the Cow

When the little gingerbread man was two days old he felt very wise.

'I know about snails and butterflies and sunshine and rain,' he said to himself. 'And I know that rain isn't good for me. What a clever little gingerbread man I am.' And he skipped and hopped along, dancing on the daisies and making the bluebells ring.

'I was made out of gingerbread, wise and strong.
I'll have a great time as I run along.
I can make bluebells ring,
I can do *anything*,
This is the gingerbread man's favourite song.'

Just then a loud, sad 'Mooooo' came from over the hedge. The gingerbread man stopped. 'Whatever can that be?' he said to himself, and stood on a mushroom to peep through the bushes. There, trapped in a large pool of black mud, was a cow.

Now, the little gingerbread man had never seen a cow. He didn't know that creatures as big as cows lived in the world. He was very frightened. 'Oh! Oh! Oh!' he squeaked, and he shivered so much that he almost fell off his mushroom.

'Mooooo!' said the cow again. 'Won't somebody help me? I fell in this bog a long time ago, and I can't get out. And all I can see is a little gingerbread man, and he is much too small to save me. Mooooo!'

At this, the little gingerbread man felt quite cross. 'Of course I can save you,' he said, and jumped off his mushroom to struggle through the hedge. But the hedge was thick and he was very small. When at last he reached the other side he had lost two of his sugar buttons and a bird had pecked crumbs from his jacket.

The cow mooed again miserably. 'Too small, too small,' she said and rolled her great head in despair.

'You won't say that when I've saved you,' said the little gingerbread man, and stood on a tussock of grass poking out of the bog. He was so light that he didn't sink in at all. 'It's a pity you're so big,' he said to the cow. 'That's what got you into trouble.'

'I was greedy,' said the cow. 'I wanted to eat the long grass that grows in the bog. And now I shall never eat anything again. Mooooo!'

'What nonsense!' The gingerbread man sprang

from his tussock of grass on to the cow's back, and from there to the firm earth of the field. He put his hands on his hips and looked about.

Far away he could see the farmhouse, which to a little gingerbread man seemed a very great distance indeed, though it was just at the edge of the field. 'I shall fetch help,' he said bravely. 'Now you will see how I can run and jump.' And at once he dashed away across the field, crying:

'Watch me run, I run so fast
That poor old cow shall be saved at last
I may be small but I'm smart and clever,
The fastest gingerbread man ever!'

The thistles had thorns as big as he was and the puddles were big enough to drown him, but the brave little gingerbread man ran on and on. At last he came to the farmhouse, and saw the kitchen door standing open. He felt a little frightened. After all, only yesterday he had run away from a house like this. But, bravely, he tiptoed inside. There sat the farmer, eating a piece of cake.

'Come with me, come with me!' cried the little
    gingerbread man.
'And you will see
What a clever gingerbread man I be!'

And he jumped up and down three times, then turned and ran from the house. At once the farmer wiped the crumbs from his chin and went after him, saying 'Well I'll be ginswoggled! If that's not a little gingerbread man!'

Away went the gingerbread man and after him went the farmer, across the field full of thistles where the puddles threatened dark and deep. Closer and closer came the farmer and the little gingerbread man was very tired. His little heart was beating against his gingerbread sides as fast as could be. The farmer's hand reached out to catch him but the little gingerbread man leaped on to a stone. He ran on faster. Again the farmer's hand reached out but the little gingerbread man ducked under a leaf. He tried to run on faster still, but he was so tired that he knew he must be caught soon. The farmer's hand reached out again.

'Cow, cow, call to me!' cried the gingerbread man, and the cow in the bog heard him.

'Mooooo,' she said, and again, 'Mooooo.'

The farmer's hand, that was just about to grab the little gingerbread man, stopped where it was. 'That sounds to me like Buttercup,' he said. 'The silly cow's got stuck in the bog.' And he went at once to pull her out.

The little gingerbread man was so tired that he flopped down in some mud. He looked down at

himself, and saw that he was muddy and messy and that some of his coat was eaten and some of his buttons lost. 'I'm still a clever little ginger-bread man,' he said and, pulling a leaf over himself for a blanket, fell fast asleep.

3

The Gingerbread Man Gets Mended

When the gingerbread man woke up the next morning, the sun was shining brightly and he felt very pleased with himself. He had been brave and helpful, and he had saved the cow even though he was far, far smaller than she was. But when he looked again at his spoiled coat and lost buttons and his muddy, messy self he didn't feel quite so happy.

'I'm not smart any more,' he said. 'I'm not nearly as crisp as when I was made.' And he sat down in the grass, leaning his head on one soggy hand.

'Hello, little gingerbread man,' said a silvery voice. It was the butterfly, shining all yellow in the morning sun. Dewdrops glittered on her wings as she rested on a leaf.

'Hello,' said the gingerbread man glumly.

'Why ever do you look so sad?' asked the butterfly. 'You were very happy when last we met.'

'You'd look sad if you'd been brave and helpful, and ended up spoiled,' said the gingerbread man. 'I'm all soggy and dirty.' Miserably he put his chin on his hand. A little piece of his mixture crumbled away and when he saw it the ginger-bread man gave a little sob. 'Soon I'll be quite gone,' he said sadly.

The butterfly fluttered into the air and came to rest on the grass beside the gingerbread man. 'Poor little gingerbread man,' she said kindly. 'Let me see if I can help you. You are the first gingerbread man I have ever seen.'

The gingerbread man was surprised by this because he thought most people were made out of gingerbread. He began to feel rather proud of himself.

'I'm glad I'm not a cloud or a butterfly or
   snail,
I'm glad I'm not a cow, or a person or a pail,
In fact if I could be whatever I chose
I'd be a gingerbread man with a gingerbread
   nose!'

And he turned a cartwheel to show that he meant it.

Meanwhile the butterfly was spreading her bright wings to the air, and fluttering them, up and down, up and down, all over the little gingerbread man. Gently, so that he didn't lose any more of his mixture, she brushed him clean. But it tickled and the gingerbread man shook

with laughter. 'Stop it! Ooh! Not there, please! Oooooh!' But the butterfly brushed on, sending mud and dirt flying away.

At last, when the gingerbread man was clean, the butterfly rested on a branch and looked at him. Little pieces were missing all over him and his edges were very soggy. 'You will soon be firm,' whispered the butterfly in her tinkly voice. 'And there are only a few pieces missing.'

'Oh dear,' said the little gingerbread man sadly. 'I see that I shall never be the same. I was made by a little old woman and there is no more of me anywhere.'

The butterfly thought for a moment. Then she rose into the air and began to flutter over the grass, dipping and swooping against the dandelions and buttercups, over the marigolds and larkspur. 'Whatever are you doing?' asked the gingerbread man, standing with his hands on his hips.

'I am gathering all your lost crumbs,' called the butterfly. 'I can see them quite clearly. In a moment we shall put you together again.'

'Hurrah! Hurrah!' cried the gingerbread man. 'Kind butterfly, good butterfly, I am sorry I was rude. You are beautiful and wise.'

At last all the gingerbread man's lost pieces were gathered. He patted the crumbs back on until his arms and his legs, his face and his feet, and all the rough places were smooth again.

'That's much better, but I still wish I had some buttons,' said the gingerbread man sadly. Then he had an idea. He bent down and picked three daisies and stuck them firmly on to his front. Then the butterfly made him lie down quite still until the sun baked him crisp.

'Now I am handsome again,' he cried, and did a little dance.

'When I was lonely I looked in the sky,
And saw high above me a big butterfly.
She cleaned me, she patted me, set me to bake;
As kind as could be for poor Gingerbread's sake.'

'Thank you, thank you, thank you!' he called to his friend. 'I am such a lucky little gingerbread man.' And he began to run over the field, leaping and bounding just like new.

4

The Gingerbread Man and the Crow

When the gingerbread man grew tired of running and jumping over the fields and the puddles and through the hedges and woods, he sat down by a stream to rest. It wasn't a very big stream but to the gingerbread man it seemed as big as a river. And he knew that on no account must he get wet because his mixture would go soft. So he sat on the bank and watched the minnows playing amongst the waterweed and he played with his new daisy buttons.

Suddenly he heard a loud, harsh noise. 'Caaark!'

He looked up. Sitting on a branch nearby was a large, black bird. 'Hello' said the gingerbread man. 'Who are you?'

'Caaark!' said the bird again. 'I'm a crow. Don't you know nothing? Where's your manners?'

'I'm sorry,' said the little gingerbread man politely 'but I've never seen a crow before. I was only baked a little while ago.'

And the crow, who actually had no manners

himself, scratched his head with a large dirty claw and said 'Seems to me a youngster like you's got no business to be out by himself.' He looked at the gingerbread man out of a large, yellow eye.

The gingerbread man began to feel a little frightened. He stood up and put his gingerbread hands behind his gingerbread back. 'I'm quite clever,' he said, 'and I can run as fast as anything. And I saved a cow.'

He didn't like to say any more because the crow had a very sharp beak and there was a gleam in his big yellow eye. And the crow's large dirty claws gripped the branch so very, very hard. The gingerbread man took a step backwards.

'Scared of me then, are you?' said the crow, and he moved along his branch.

'No of course not,' said the gingerbread man, and he took another step back.

'What's the harm in a little chitchat on a fine spring morning?' said the crow, and again he moved along his branch towards the gingerbread man.

'Nothing, I'm sure,' said the gingerbread man, and this time he went back two steps very quickly.

'And what could be nicer than a nice little gingerbread man for breakfast?' said the crow

and he stretched his claws and flapped his wings
and sprang into the air.

'Oh! Oh! Oh!' shrieked the gingerbread man
and he turned and ran as fast as his little gingerbread legs would go. The stream at his side
gurgled, 'Run, run little gingerbread man or the
crow will eat you' and the little fishes playing in
the waterweed whispered 'Run, run little gingerbread man!' And the gingerbread man ran,
bounding and leaping over the grass and the
stones, the twigs and the flowers.

'Caaark! Caaark!' called the crow trying to grab the little gingerbread man in his claws as he flew.

'Oh! Oh!' cried the gingerbread man. 'Where can I hide?'

But there was nowhere to hide. On one side was the stream and on the other the wide, flat field. He made a great leap and then another, for he could hear the crow getting closer. 'Caaark! Caaark!'

The gingerbread man looked up and saw the crow's black, beating wings. With a frightened shriek he leapt into the stream. 'Caaark!' called the crow angrily. 'Caaark!' And he flew off to find something else for breakfast.

And that should have been the end of the gingerbread man. But – there wasn't a splash. Where *had* the gingerbread man gone? The crow couldn't see him and the little fishes couldn't find him. And do you know why? Because he had jumped right into the middle of a lilypad, growing in the steam, and the lily flower had closed right up over him to keep him safe.

'Phew!' said the gingerbread man, climbing out of the flower. 'That was close. Thank you, kind flower, for saving me. But now what am I to do? I cannot swim and I cannot reach the shore. I shall have to stay on this lilypad for ever!' Tired from his running and very sad, he sat down on

the pad and rested his chin on his hands.

'Never mind,' whispered the fishes. 'Never mind little gingerbread man.' And to cheer himself up the gingerbread man sang himself a little song:

'I'm a gingerbread man, just look and see,
That bad old crow thought he'd gobble gobble me,
But I ran and I jumped and I tried to hide
And the kind lily flower let me inside.'

'You're a beautiful flower,' said the gingerbread man and the lily cradled him in her lovely pink-white petals. And the fishes whispered and the stream sang a lullaby, and in the heat of the day the gingerbread man went fast asleep.

5

The Gingerbread Man
and the Rescue

When the gingerbread man woke up and found himself still trapped on his lilypad he was quite upset at first. But then he thought of how much he had managed to do so far in his short, gingerbread life. And he said to himself, 'I shall manage somehow. I'm the cleverest, strongest, most handsome gingerbread man in the world!' But he didn't say it as loudly as he had when he was first made, because he had learned to be sensible.

Looking about him he saw that a large, green frog sat on a neighbouring lilypad. 'How do you do?' said the gingerbread man politely.

'Croak,' said the frog. And then again 'Croak.'

'Can't you say anything else?' asked the gingerbread man.

'Croak,' said the frog in reply. And he leapt off the lilypad and swam away across the stream, his long, frog legs sending him swiftly through the water.

'I wish I could swim,' said the gingerbread

man, but he knew that he dared not even get wet, because his mixture would go soft. And he knew too that he had to be careful about asking for help, because he was very good to eat. But he also knew that he was really quite clever.

He noticed that one of the lilyflower's petals was lying by itself on the lilypad, a beautiful pink-white shell. The gingerbread man tried sitting in it, and it was only a little bit small. His ginger bottom fitted very snugly into the petal.

'I think this might be the answer,' said the gingerbread man to himself, and he sang himself a little song to help him feel brave:

'I'm a gingerbread man in a terrible fix,
I've not seen such trouble since when I was
    mixed,
But now I shall sit in the petal so small
And float to the side with no worries at all!'

So, carefully, he climbed out of the petal, carried it to the edge of the lilypad and floated it on the water. Then he said, 'Goodbye, kind lilypad. I am off on a great adventure.' And once again he sat himself in the petal and pushed off into the wide waters of the stream.

At once he found that sailing in boats was difficult. The petal went round and round in the current, and the gentle breeze blew it this way and that. It did not go to the bank as the gingerbread man had thought it would, but rushed down the stream, on and on, through the ripples and eddies, round the rocks and the little stone islands.

'Oh! Oh! Oh!' cried the little gingerbread man, and the stream and the fishes whispered 'Oh! Oh! Oh!' as he was swept quickly along. There was a branch lying across the stream. The petal was flung against it, and for a moment the gingerbread man thought he was lost. He put up his gingerbread arms to keep the twigs from scratching him, and one piece of a twig came off in his hand. The petal rushed on.

'Now I have something to help me,' said the gingerbread man bravely, and he put his twig into the water, to steer his petal and to push against stones and rocks.

On and on they went. The stream seemed to be flowing faster and faster, but the brave little gingerbread man held tight to his twig and tried again and again to steer to the bank. But the water was rushing too quickly.

'Help! Help!' Above the splashing of the stream, the gingerbread man could hear a small, frightened voice. He looked around to see who it might be.

'Help! Help!' There, on a tiny pebble sticking out of the rushing waters of the stream, was a harvest mouse. He was clinging on tightly but it seemed that at any moment he would fall into the water, and he was very wet already. His long, slender tail was wrapped around his little fat body and he looked very unhappy.

'Hold on! I'm coming!' The gingerbread man pushed hard with his twig and sent his petal boat racing towards the mouse. As soon as the boat came near the stone the little mouse leaped aboard, and rocking wildly, the boat went on its headlong way.

Carrying both a mouse and a gingerbread man the petal was very full indeed. The mouse sat sobbing and holding his tail while the ginger-

bread man fought to save them both. At last, with a mighty effort, he pushed the little boat to the bank. They both scrambled out and lay panting on the grass.

'Thank you! Thank you!' gasped the mouse. 'I was sitting on a corn stalk and the wind blew me into the stream. I should have drowned straight away if I had not found the stone, and then if you had not saved me as you did my family would have been without me forever! I must return to them. I shall go at once.'

'It's a very long way,' said the gingerbread man, looking at the long length of the stream which they had rushed down so quickly in their petal boat.

The mouse gripped his tail with his little hands. 'I know that,' he said bravely. 'I will start at once. Thank you and goodbye.' Brushing the last of the water from his whiskers, the little mouse started on his long and dangerous journey.

The gingerbread man stood looking after him. Such a very small mouse with such a very long way to go.

'What he needs is a clever little gingerbread man to help him,' said the gingerbread man. 'Wait for me, Mouse! I'm coming!' And the gingerbread man ran after him, singing his song:

'I'm a gingerbread man, just look and see,
I'm really quite clever as clever can be.
I run so fast, I jump so high,
One day I just might touch the sky!'

And off he ran, bouncing and skipping, to find
even more adventures.

6

The Gingerbread Man
Feels Hungry

When the gingerbread man and the mouse began their journey they were both quite tired. And as they walked and walked along the river bank they soon became quite hungry.

'I wish I had something to eat,' said the little gingerbread man, and he flopped down on to a pebble.

'I am hungry too,' said the mouse and at once he began to gather pieces of grass and leaves. He gave some to the gingerbread man and sat down himself, munching happily.

The gingerbread man nibbled a little piece of grass. 'It really tastes very strange,' he said, watching the mouse eat up all his leaves as well. The gingerbread man tried a piece of leaf, but that tasted just as horrid as the grass.

'Delicious!' said the mouse, rubbing his full tummy.

'I don't think gingerbread men are supposed to eat grass and leaves,' said the gingerbread man. 'And I am so very hungry!' He got up and began to look around to see if he could find something else to eat. Low down in the hedge were some pretty red berries. 'Look at these!' he cried gleefully. 'They are so pretty that they must be good to eat.' And he seized a berry and opened his mouth to bite into it.

'Stop! Stop!' squeaked the mouse, his whiskers quivering with fright.

The gingerbread man looked at him crossly. 'Why are you stopping me?' he asked. 'I'm hungry.'

'Those berries will make you very, very ill,' gasped the mouse. 'My mother taught me never to eat them, and I have taught my children, each and every one of them. Don't eat them, little gingerbread man.'

The gingerbread man didn't know about being ill, but it didn't sound very nice. He put the berry down. 'All right,' he said. 'But what can I eat? There is nothing here that tastes good to a gingerbread man.'

'Caaark! Caaark!' came a harsh voice from high up above them. 'I see something that will taste very good to me.' It was the crow.

'Run! Run for your life!' cried the gingerbread man, and he and the mouse jumped and leapt and scampered. The crow flew down, his dirty yellow claws reaching out to catch them. Hither and thither they ran, this way and that, and the crow's black wings cast a shadow so big that it blotted out the sun.

'We shall be caught! We shall be eaten by a crow!' squeaked the little harvest mouse, and he rolled into a ball on the ground, quivering with fright.

But just then the little gingerbread man saw a tiny hole in the ground. He popped inside it, only to see the crow reaching down to grab his friend the mouse.

'Tasty mouse for my dinner! Who needs a little gingerbread man?' croaked the crow.

At once the little gingerbread man leapt from his hole and grabbed the mouse's long tail in his little gingerbread hand. A mighty heave – and the gingerbread man and the mouse were safe in their hole.

The crow stood on the ground outside, his yellow claws blocking the entrance. 'Come out, little gingerbread man, come out, little mouse,' said the crow in a sly voice. 'Nice chap like me's not going to hurt you.'

Safe in his hole the gingerbread man spoke up bravely. 'You're not nice,' he said in a loud voice. 'Go away, Crow, and find your supper elsewhere!'

And at last, when the crow saw that the gingerbread man was not going to come out of the hole, he flew away hungry to a dead tree, and sat there, combing his dirty feathers with his claws.

After a while, the gingerbread man and the mouse climbed out of the hole and looked about them. 'I'm hungrier than ever,' said the gingerbread man. 'What can I eat, Mouse? What should I like?'

Whiskers quivering, the mouse ran to the hedge and quickly climbed up into it, searching amongst the prickles and the branches.

'What are you looking for?' asked the gingerbread man, watching from below.

'Catch!' called the mouse. And down fell fat berries, big and purple and full of juice.

'Are these good to eat?' asked the gingerbread man, who was beginning to think he would never find anything nice.

'Try them,' called the mouse. 'They are called blackberries.'

So the gingerbread man put the berries in his mouth. They tasted nicer than almost anything, and he ate berry after berry, until his mouth had turned quite purple.

'Now I've found something I like!' he said happily, and did a little dance of joy.

'A gingerbread man should never be
As empty as empty as empty can be,
He should sing in the sun and always be
  merry,
And never forget the tasty blackberry!'

And off went the mouse and the gingerbread man once again.

7

The Gingerbread Man
Meets a Fox

As the gingerbread man and the mouse went along, the gingerbread man boasted about all his adventures. 'I have seen a great many things,' he said proudly. 'And I shall certainly see a great many more. I tell you this, little mouse, there is only one thing to be frightened of, and that is the crow.'

The mouse combed his quivering whiskers. 'I really don't know about that,' he said shyly. 'It seems to me that there are very many frightening things in the world. I am very often frightened myself.'

But the gingerbread man laughed and danced about, saying, 'What a timid little mouse you are. If you were a gingerbread man you would be very much braver.

'I'm a gingerbread man, just look and see,
There's no one in the world as clever as me,
I run so fast, I jump so high,
Quite soon I'll even touch the sky!'

For the day was sunny and warm and the little gingerbread man had forgotten all the times when he hadn't thought he was quite so clever.

Just then the sun went behind a cloud. The little mouse shivered. 'I think it's going to rain,' he said in his timid little voice.

'Oh dear! Do you think so?' said the gingerbread man. 'We must shelter at once. For I am made out of gingerbread and I mustn't get wet.'

They hurried along the path, looking for somewhere to shelter. There wasn't anywhere, not a hole or a cave, or even a place where the leaves hung down thick over the ground.

'What shall I do, what shall I do?' cried the gingerbread man, wringing his gingerbread hands.

'Quickly! Over here.' The mouse was scurrying about beneath a hedge.

Just as the first drops of rain began to fall, the gingerbread man and the mouse found shelter in a mossy nook under the hawthorn.

All around the rain fell, whispering on to the leaves and branches. 'I like it here,' said the gingerbread man, watching the water fall like a curtain spread across the air.

'So do I,' said a voice. 'It really is very pleasant.' The gingerbread man looked at the mouse. 'Did you say that?' he asked. 'It didn't sound like you.'

'I don't think it was me,' said the mouse, but he pulled one of his whiskers down and stared at it, in case his whiskers were muttering things.

'It was me,' said a voice behind them.

They both turned round. Sitting quite comfortably in the moss was a large red animal, with a pointed nose, white teeth, bright eyes and a great big, bushy red tail. She was very beautiful and the gingerbread man felt quite cross, because he had thought he was the most handsome thing in the world. As they watched, the creature put out her red tongue and licked all around her mouth. The mouse squeaked and tried to hide behind the gingerbread man. The gingerbread man would have liked to hide behind the mouse, but he didn't want to show he was frightened, so he said, 'Hello. Who are you?'

'I,' said the creature, yawning and showing her pointed teeth, 'am a fox. A very beautiful fox. You, I see, are a gingerbread man, and very foolish indeed.'

'I am certainly not foolish,' said the gingerbread man crossly. 'I'm the cleverest gingerbread man there is.'

Again the fox yawned and wrapped her great tail more cosily round her toes. 'Don't you know,

little man, that foxes eat gingerbread? They like it very, very much.'

Then the little gingerbread man quivered with fright, but still he did not show it. 'Is that so?' he said bravely. 'Then why aren't you eating me now?'

'Because I'm not hungry,' said the fox, and lay down with a sly smile on her foxy face. 'But I will be. And when I feel that I should like a tasty little gingerbread man I shall gobble you up all in one go. I might even take some crumbs home to my den for the children. I have several children and they are all' – she yawned again – 'beautiful. They take after me of course.'

Now the little gingerbread man realized he was going to have to be very clever indeed if he was to escape being eaten by the fox. So he sat down on the mossy ground and put his chin in his hands to think. The mouse, who was shivering so much that his teeth rattled, moaned, 'I know I shall never see my home again. My wife and my children! Ohhh!'

'Shhh!' whispered the gingerbread man. 'I have a plan.'

He stood up and went over to the fox, who was snoozing with her bright eyes half closed. 'Mrs Fox,' said the gingerbread man politely, 'I am getting tired of waiting to be eaten. Do you think we could play a game to pass the time?'

'What sort of game?' said the fox, flicking her long red tail this way and that.

'Hide and seek,' said the gingerbread man. 'My friend the mouse will hide in this hedge and you and I will look for him.'

'You will escape,' said the fox and licked her chops.

'Of course I shall not! A gingerbread man dare not go out in the rain and it is raining very, very hard,' said the little gingerbread man.

'How true,' said the fox, 'how true. Let us begin! And if I find the little mouse I shall bite him!'

At this, the mouse squeaked and ran amongst the hawthorn branches, in and out, this way and that, swinging from twig to twig on his long bare tail.

'I see him! I shall catch him!' cried the fox, and jumped after the mouse. But the hawthorn branches were very prickly, and all the fox got for her pains was a prickled nose.

'Let me, let me!' shouted the gingerbread man, and hopped and skipped after the mouse, up and up into the hedge. Soon he reached the mouse, and taking one tiny paw in his own gingerbread hand he called 'Now we shall see who is foolish! Jump, Mouse, jump!' And the little gingerbread man and the mouse leapt out of the hedge and into the rain.

It ought to have been very horrid for the gingerbread man, who should have gone all soggy. But what did he hold up high over his head? A great big leaf that he had found on the ground under the hedge, and the rain bounced off it just as if the little gingerbread man was under an umbrella. The little gingerbread man and the mouse scampered off to safety through the rain.

'I have been tricked!' cried the fox, and gnashed her white teeth in rage.

And the little gingerbread man ran along under his leaf and sang a song:

'I'm a gingerbread man, as brave as can be,
Not even a fox can worry, worry me,
Watch me jump, watch me run, just see if you can,
I'm the bravest and cleverest gingerbread man.'

'I shall catch you one day, little gingerbread man,' said the fox, and lay down again on the moss.

8

The Gingerbread Man
and the Harvest Mice

After the gingerbread man and the mouse had been travelling for a long, long time, the mouse began to sniff and snuffle in the grass beside the path.

'Whatever is the matter?' asked the gingerbread man. 'Why are you sniffing and snuffling? Is there something strange in the grass?'

The mouse looked up and there was an excited expression in his little black eyes. 'It is just that this grass smells to me like my own grass. The grass near my home. I do believe, little gingerbread man, that if we go along a little further we shall come to my own, my very own cornfield, and that there we shall find my own dear wife and children!'

The gingerbread man jumped up and down, clapping his gingerbread hands. 'I have brought you home, just as I promised! Let us run and jump and scamper along the way.

'When poor harvest mouse was lost and alone
And far, far away from his own little home,

The gingerbread man helped him find the
  way
He'll be back with his wife and children
  today.

'Where are your wife and family, Mouse? Show
me where you live.'

At this the little mouse scampered across the
grass and the gingerbread man jumped and
skipped after him. They came to a great wall of
yellow corn, waving tall and thick in the warm
summer breeze. 'This is my home!' cried the
mouse and at once disappeared into the
cornfield.

'Where are you? I cannot see you!' cried the
gingerbread man, and he tried to run after the
mouse, but he kept bumping into thick stems
of corn.

'I am here! Up here!' called the mouse and,
looking up, the gingerbread man could see the
mouse swinging amongst the corn stalks by his
tail and little pink paws. He stopped at a round
ball of grass, hanging between two strong stems.
'My dear! I have returned,' called the mouse, and
at once his wife and children climbed out of their
little nest of grass to welcome him.

There was such a squeaking and crying and
hugging that the gingerbread man felt a little shy.
He thought it might be best if he went away

quietly now that the mouse was safe once again, and he began to sneak away through the corn.

'Wait! Wait, little gingerbread man!' The mouse had remembered him and swung down from his cornstalk. 'You must stay with us,' said the mouse. 'For you have run away from your home and have nowhere to live.'

'I ran away from a little old woman,' said the gingerbread man. 'But I have run and jumped ever since. Do I need a home?'

'Everybody needs a home,' said the mouse and took the little gingerbread man up the cornstalk to his nest of grass. Mrs Mouse and all the little mice stood in a shy row on an ear of corn. 'Hello', 'Hello', 'Hello', 'Hello', 'Hello', they said one after the other. And Mrs Mouse said, 'Do come in.'

So the gingerbread man went into the little nest, hanging high above the ground. It seemed very small but very warm and cosy. Then all the mice came in too, and it seemed even smaller. In fact it was so small that the little gingerbread man found every part of him had a mouse sitting on it!

'Somebody is nibbling me!' he cried suddenly. 'Somebody is nibbling my toe!'

Then Mrs Mouse turned round and scolded one of the little mice so hard that he began to cry. 'But Ma,' he wailed, 'he tastes so good!'

The little gingerbread man saw that the mouse's home was no place for him. It was too small, and the baby mice would nibble him. He squeezed carefully out once again and said goodbye to his friend. 'I must go on my travels,' he said. 'For I think that's the proper life for a gingerbread man.'

But before he could set off on his way, there came a terrible rumbling and crashing in the cornfield.

'What is it? What is happening?' asked the gingerbread man.

'Wife! Children! Come at once!' called the mouse. Straight away, all the mice began to scamper and swing to the edge of the cornfield. The gingerbread man went with them, and they sat together under the hedge, the little mice all squeaking and Mrs Mouse gathering them safe to her side.

'It is the farmer with his machine,' said the mouse sombrely. 'Every year they come and take the corn. Now we must build a new home. Stay with us, little gingerbread man, we will build a home big enough for us all.'

But the little gingerbread man didn't like the cornfield and the farmer's great machine, that roared and chewed up the corn and the home of the little mice. 'This isn't the place for me,' he said firmly. After that he said goodbye to his friend the mouse, and to Mrs Mouse and all the little mice. 'Goodbye', 'Goodbye', 'Goodbye', 'Goodbye', 'Goodbye', they replied, and the little gingerbread man hopped and skipped away, through the hedge, over the tussocky grass, away from the cornfields and off to the heath and the woodland beyond.

9

The Gingerbread Man in the Night

After quite a lot of running and jumping, the gingerbread man came to a wood, full of tall trees and deep shadows. He saw that it was getting dark. The evening air was becoming damp and chill.

'I must find somewhere to rest,' said the gingerbread man. 'Perhaps I should have stayed with the mouse after all, only I am sure that I should have woken in the morning to find myself nibbled all away. There will be somewhere warm and dry in this wood.'

So off went the gingerbread man into the wood. Under the trees it seemed very dark indeed. The gingerbread man began to feel a little frightened. 'Twit Twooooo' came a great loud hoot overhead, and the gingerbread man pressed himself back against a tree and looked up at the huge white owl that flew in the dark air above him.

'What are you doooooing here, little ginger-bread man?' said the owl, flapping his wide white wings. 'Don't you know that Fox is abroad in the wood at night? And Fox likes nothing better than gingerbread men.'

'Oh, I've met Fox before,' said the gingerbread man, 'and she didn't frighten me one bit.' And he jigged up and down to show just how brave he was.

'What a foolish gingerbread man,' said the owl. 'But I cannot stay and talk. I am going hunt ... hunt ... hunting!' And the owl swooped away across the treetops into the night sky, hooting as he went. 'Twit Twooo. Twit Twooo. Twit Twooooooooo.'

The little gingerbread man continued on his way. Despite what he had said to the owl, he was a little frightened. The wood was full of noises and shadows, and he began to think that every dark place hid the red fox, with her beautiful white teeth and long bushy tail. So he sang a little song to make him feel brave again:

'I'm a gingerbread man, alone in the night,
The owl came and hooted and gave me a fright,
He said that red fox is abroad in the wood,
But I'll run and I'll jump like Gingerbread should!'

And he scampered on through the trees, hopping between the bushes and jumping over twigs and holes. He didn't notice the bright eyes that watched him, the stoats and the weasels that saw him pass. But he did see old Badger, snuffling his way along.

'Hello,' said the gingerbread man, stopping. 'May I say, sir, what a smart black and white coat you are wearing?' For the gingerbread man did remember his manners sometimes.

'Why – thank you, young fella,' said the badger, peering down at him. 'What's a young chap like you doing out in the night, hmmm? Don't you know Red Fox is looking for some

supper for her children? They'd like a bit of gingerbread I'm sure.'

'I've met the red fox before and she didn't eat me then,' said the gingerbread man proudly. 'This wood is very dark, isn't it? And there aren't many people to talk to.'

'But they are all around you,' said the badger. 'Stoat! Weasel! Bat! Come and show yourselves to this gingerbread man.' And then he snuffled off through the trees.

There came a rustling in the leaves and branches, and bright eyes peeped out from the shadows. The gingerbread man put his hands behind his back and shivered.

'Hello,' said long Stoat, gliding into view.

'Hello,' said little Weasel, coming quick, quick after him.

'Hello,' squeaked Bat, swooping noiselessly in the night air.

'How do you do?' said the little gingerbread man. 'I am looking for somewhere warm and dry where I may rest for a time. Do any of you kind people know of a place?'

'We can't spare the time to talk to you,' said the stoat, moving his thin flat head this way and that.

'We are hunting,' agreed the weasel, and the bat squeaked, 'It must all be done before morning!'

'Oh dear,' said the gingerbread man, 'whatever shall I do? I must find somewhere warm, the night is so cold and dark.'

Just then the bushes parted. They heard a soft footfall. The stoat and the weasel and the bat turned and fled quite away, as the red fox stepped out into the moonlight. 'Hello, little gingerbread man' she said, licking her beautiful red whiskers.

'Hello,' said the gingerbread man, but he stepped quickly backwards. The fox held up one red paw. 'Don't run away. Come with me to my den, it's warm and dry and cosy. You can meet my children.'

'But you want to eat me,' said the gingerbread man, and at this the fox laughed merrily, showing her sharp white teeth.

'Of course I shall not eat you, little gingerbread man! How foolish you are.'

Now the little gingerbread man didn't like it when people said he was foolish. At once he put his hands on his hips and cried:

'I'm a gingerbread man and clever as can be,
And you Red Fox you don't fool me,
I'll run and I'll jump away from this place,
And you won't catch me however you chase.'

And he turned and scampered away. All around the night creatures whispered, 'Run! Run little gingerbread man,' and he ran, while the fox dashed after him, her whiskers on end and her red legs racing.

The gingerbread man began to feel very tired. It was dark and he couldn't see where he was going. Behind him he could hear the fox's legs padding along the ground. 'I am going to be caught!' he cried. 'What shall I do?'

'Up here, up here, little gingerbread man!' squeaked a voice, and looking up the gingerbread man saw the bat, sitting on the branch of a tree.

At once the gingerbread man took a deep breath and jumped as high as ever he could. He just managed to scramble up. At the foot of the tree he could hear the red fox searching, muttering to herself, 'Where is that tasty little gingerbread man? What shall my children eat now for their supper?' And he was very glad indeed that he had not gone to Red Fox's den.

'You may sleep here if you like,' said the bat, fluttering about the gingerbread man's head.

'Thank you,' said the gingerbread man, looking around the branch. It was bare, with hardly any leaves. 'But how shall I sleep?'

'Like this, of course,' said the bat, and turned upside down, hooking his feet over the branch. His head hung down beside the gingerbread man and looked very odd indeed, and he folded

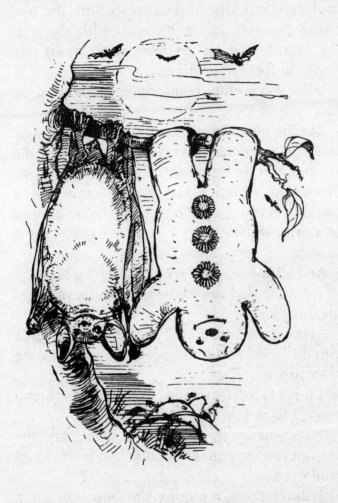

his wings round him like a cloak.

'How very strange,' said the gingerbread man. 'But it was very kind of you to rescue me, Bat, and I shall certainly try.' So he hooked his legs over the branch and let his head hang down. He began to feel rather dizzy.

'Now you see how comfortable this is,' said the bat.

But the gingerbread man wasn't comfortable at all. He seemed a very long way from the ground and he didn't feel safe hanging upside down from a branch. He closed his eyes but he couldn't get to sleep, not even when he hooked one arm and one leg over the branch for a change.

And all the time the bat was sleeping happily, his wings folded round his body and a smile on his furry face.

At last it was morning. The sun shone brightly into the wood and it did not seem a frightening place any more.

'I think I shall leave now,' said the gingerbread man. 'Thank you very much, Bat.'

'Now you see the best way to sleep,' said the bat, not properly awake because bats like to sleep until evening.

'I don't think it's quite the best way for a gingerbread man,' said the little gingerbread man, trying not to yawn. And off he went through the wood, running and jumping, out into the fields and the sunshine.

10

The Gingerbread Man
Catches Cold

All through the morning the gingerbread man ran and jumped in the sunshine. But after a while he began to feel rather strange. His throat felt hot and there was a tickly feeling in his nose. When he sat down on a stone to rest, his nose began to tickle very, very much and suddenly it screwed up tight and the gingerbread man said 'A-TISHOO!!!' very, very loudly.

'What is happening to me?' cried the gingerbread man. 'My nose won't behave itself!' And before he could do anything about it his nose screwed up again and said an even bigger 'A-TISHOO!!!'

The gingerbread man began to feel rather sorry for himself. 'This is what comes of sleeping upside down,' he said. 'My nose is cross with me and won't behave.' But his throat felt even hotter and there was a horrid ache in his head. The gingerbread man went slowly and sadly to sit under a tree in the shade.

'Caark! Caark!' Suddenly a big black bird

hopped on the grass in front of him. It was the crow, with a sharp look in his beady yellow eyes. 'Now I've got you, little gingerbread man,' he said and put out his yellow claws to grab him.

'A-TISHOO!!!' said the little gingerbread man. The crow hopped backwards.

'What's that you say? Something the matter is there?' croaked the crow and he put his head on one side. All his dirty feathers stood up in spikes.

'A-TISHOO!!!' said the gingerbread man once more, for he really couldn't say anything else.

The crow hopped back still further. 'Caark! Caark! I knows what you've got. By my fleas, you've got a cold. Caark! Caark! Keep away, or I shall peck you. I don't want to catch it.'

'What's a cold?' asked the gingerbread man, and his voice sounded funny.

'What is it? It's what you've got. And you ain't got no respect for your betters. What's my missus going to say if I gets a cold? Keep away, keep away! Nothing but trouble, that's you.' And flapping his wings crossly the crow flew off into a tree. He sat all hunched up, coughing from time to time and muttering 'I know I'll catch it. Blast that little gingerbread man.'

But the little gingerbread man felt too ill to notice. He plodded off slowly through the grass, trying to sing a little song to cheer himself up:

69

'I'm a gingerbread man in rather a stew,
My nose keeps going A-A-A-TISHOO!!
I haven't a friend, I've nowhere to go,
I'm a sad little gingerbread man – I am so!'

But it didn't cheer him up at all.

Just then a low, slow voice said 'Whatever is the matter, little gingerbread man?'

Looking down into the grass the gingerbread man saw the snail, peeping out of his shell.

'Hello Snail,' said the gingerbread man miserably. 'I've got a cold. Not even the crow will speak to me, so you'd better crawl away quickly before you start going "A-A-A-TISHOO!!" as well.'

The snail gave a low, slow, chuckle. 'Is that all? A cold isn't so terrible, little man, in a few days it will be quite, quite gone. And besides, snails don't catch colds.'

'But I thought I should be like this for ever,' said the gingerbread man, beginning to feel a little better. 'And my throat is so sore and my head so hot, and sometimes it's my head that's sore and my throat that's hot. A-TISHOO, A-TISHOO!!! What shall I do, snail?'

The snail thought for a moment. 'It seems to me that Mrs Rabbit is the person to help you,' he said at last. 'Stay here, Gingerbread Man, and I shall fetch her.'

So while the gingerbread man sat all hunched up on a stone the snail crawled off over the grass, leaving his slimy, silvery trail and seeing the way with his big horns and feeling the way with his little ones.

It seemed a very long time that he was gone. The gingerbread man sneezed and sneezed, and when he tried to sing to himself it came out just like the crow's 'Caark! Caark!' which he didn't like at all.

Suddenly there was a thump, thump on the ground and there in front of him was Mrs Rabbit.

'What a state you're in, little gingerbread man,' she said in her motherly way. 'I shall have to take you to my burrow, that I can see.'

'I've got a cold,' croaked the gingerbread man sadly. And the rabbit said, 'As if I can't see that! Warm blackberry juice is what you need, and a nice cosy nest to lie in. Come along, come along!' And she pushed the gingerbread man with her soft furry nose. He trudged off down the path, not jumping and skipping at all.

When they reached the burrow, all the little rabbits popped out and looked at him. 'It's a gingerbread man, it's a gingerbread man,' they whispered. But their mother said crossly 'Go off at once, children, and play. This gingerbread man's got a cold.'

'A-TISHOO!!' said the gingerbread man. And again, 'A-TISHOO!!'

But in no time at all Mrs Rabbit had him tucked up warm, with a handkerchief of rabbit fur and a drink of blackberry juice. The gingerbread man began to think that perhaps it wasn't so bad having a cold and he sang a little croaky song to himself:

'I'm a gingerbread man, who's not very well,
How lucky I was to meet that old snail,
And now Mrs Rabbit has tucked me in bed,
And put a soft pillow at Gingerbread's head!

'I'm sure I shall be better in the morning,' he murmured, and snuggled down in the warm rabbit burrow to go to sleep.

11

The Gingerbread Man
Has a Narrow Escape

The next day the gingerbread man felt so much better that he jumped out of bed and skipped to the top of the burrow. The sun was shining.

'Thank you, thank you, thank you Mrs Rabbit,' he called, jumping on the short grass and making all the little rabbits hop about in excitement. 'I'm better! I'm well! My nose is behaving itself!'

'Just make sure you sleep the right way up from now on,' said Mrs Rabbit, and the gingerbread man laughed, dashing this way and that because he was so pleased with himself.

'I must go and say thank you to the snail,' he said, and he began to run across the fields, calling 'Snail! Snail! Where are you? Are you asleep on this lovely morning?'

The snail poked his horns out of his house. 'Who is making such a noise so early?' he asked, yawning. 'Oh, it's you, little gingerbread man. Are you better?'

'Yes I am,' said the gingerbread man. 'I'm good as new. Thank you for taking care of me.'

'You just be careful, little gingerbread man. A little man like you could get himself eaten.'

At this the gingerbread man laughed merrily. 'I shan't be eaten!' he declared. 'I know everything now!

'I'm a gingerbread man, just look and see,
There's no one in the world as clever as me,
I run so fast, I jump so high,
Quite soon I'll even touch the sky!'

And the snail shook his head and muttered 'You'll learn, little man, you'll learn.'

But the little gingerbread man really did think he knew everything, and he ran across the fields and the tussocky grass full of pride and happiness. He said to himself 'I mustn't touch puddles because I'll go soggy. I mustn't eat berries because I shall feel bad. And I mustn't sleep upside down because then I shall catch a horrid, horrid cold. But I can do anything else I like!' And he danced on a toadstool just to show he could.

Just then he heard a dreadful squeaking. 'Whatever can that be?' he said to himself, and still standing on the toadstool he put his hands on his hips and looked all about him. And what should he see but Mrs Fox, running across the grass after one of the baby rabbits!

'I shall bite you! I shall bite you and take you

home to my children,' called the fox. And the baby rabbit ran faster and squeaked 'Oh! Oh! Oh!'

Without thinking twice, the gingerbread man dashed between the fox and the rabbit. Bravely he shouted:

'I'm a gingerbread man and I taste very good
Will little fox like me like little fox should?
Come chase me, come catch me, just see if
  you can,
I'm the tastiest raciest gingerbread man!'

And away he dashed while the little rabbit ran off home to his mother.

'Gingerbread Man! By my beautiful red whiskers I should like to taste you,' said the fox, showing her bright white teeth. At once she began to chase after him, her red legs racing.

After a little time, the gingerbread man looked over his shoulder and saw that the fox was not very near. 'She can't catch me,' he said proudly, and thought that he would stop running very soon. After a little time more, he looked over his shoulder and saw that the fox was quite a lot nearer. 'I don't *think* she'll catch me,' he said, not quite so proudly, and thought that he wouldn't stop running just yet. And after a little time more, he looked over his shoulder and saw that the fox was almost on top of him. 'Oh dear! Oh

dear! What shall I do?' he cried. 'The fox is going to eat me!'

The crow, sitting in a tree combing his dirty feathers, heard the little gingerbread man. 'What's that you say? The fox will eat the gingerbread man? Oh no she don't, that gingerbread man's meant for me!' And with an angry 'Caark! Caark!' the crow flapped noisily off his branch.

'Go away!' cried the fox, snapping her white teeth. 'I have chased the gingerbread man and I shall eat him.'

'I saw him first. He's mine!' croaked the crow, and scratched at the fox with dirty yellow claws.

'He's mine!' snapped the fox.

'He's mine!' croaked the crow, and they snapped and scratched, snapped and scratched, quite forgetting the gingerbread man.

The little gingerbread man crept away into the bushes. He chuckled to himself. 'I don't think I want to be eaten,' he said happily, and went on his way in the sunshine and the warm summer breeze.

12

The Gingerbread Man Gets Prickled

While the gingerbread man ran along, he thought to himself how pretty the world was with its flowers of yellow and white and blue, its bright berries and green leaves and the lovely, fluttery butterflies. He thought it sounded good too, for a blackbird was singing and the harebells made ringing sounds as the wind blew them. 'No wonder I am in the world,' he said to himself. 'I am such a handsome gingerbread man.'

Just then he heard a snuffling, snorting sound and out of the undergrowth came the strangest creature. It had a long, piggy nose, bright eyes and prickles all over its back. As it went it snuffled up grubs and beetles and gobbled them down. The gingerbread man stared. 'Who are you?' he asked, rather rudely.

'I might ask the same question,' said the creature. 'I'm Hedgehog. Who are you?'

'I'm the little gingerbread man,' said the gingerbread man in surprise. 'You must surely have heard of me.'

'Can't say as I have,' said the hedgehog, and

started off on his snuffling way again.

'Wait!' called the gingerbread man. 'Where are you going?'

The hedgehog stopped and looked back. 'I'm going to the gardens. Want to come? Always a bowl of bread and milk waiting.'

And since the gingerbread man was rather hungry, off he went.

Soon they came to a thick, tall hedge. The hedgehog went snuffling to a hole and wriggled through, and after him squeezed the gingerbread man. On the other side was a smooth grass lawn, a pond with fish in it, and lots and lots of beautiful big flowers.

'What a very strange place,' said the gingerbread man. 'Is this a safe place to be?'

The hedgehog shrugged. 'Can't say as I know. Safe enough for a hedgehog, that's for sure. Look, here's the bread and milk, over here in this blue bowl.' And off he snuffled with the gingerbread man close behind.

Somehow, even though the bread and milk tasted lovely, the gingerbread man felt nervous. The garden was so quiet. There wasn't even the sound of harebells ringing. So he sang a little song to make himself brave:

'When I was alone in the fields one fine day,
I met a strange creature who brought me this way.

We came to a garden and found something
   good,
And I said a brave thank you, like Gingerbread should.'

But he didn't feel very much braver. The garden
still seemed very strange with only the gingerbread man and the hedgehog in it. The gingerbread man wondered if there might be someone
– he didn't know who – watching him.

'I think I'll go now,' he said loudly to the
hedgehog.

'Just as you please,' said the hedgehog,
snuffling right to the bottom of the bowl.

'It's not that I'm frightened or anything,' said
the gingerbread man. 'But I have to be on my
way.'

'Do as you like,' said the hedgehog, licking all
round the sides of the bowl.

'So I'll be off then,' said the gingerbread man.
But before he could do anything at all, what
should he see coming towards him? A great big
man with a beard, crying, 'I'll catch it! I'll catch
the little creature!'

'Oh! Oh! Oh!' cried the gingerbread man. 'I
shall be caught! Hedgehog, what shall I do?' But
when he looked round for the hedgehog, he was
nowhere to be seen! All that was there was a tight
ball of prickles, the same colour as the hedgehog

but now all round and sharp.

'Where are you?' cried the gingerbread man, and from the prickles came a muffled voice. 'Go away, Gingerbread Man. Go away.'

'Let me in, let me in,' called the gingerbread man, and he tried to find his way into the prickles so that he could hide with the hedgehog. But he couldn't find the hedgehog's head, or his tail, or his legs, and he certainly couldn't find a way into the ball of prickles. What he did find was that his gingerbread hands began to hurt very much.

'I've been prickled,' cried the gingerbread man. 'Oh! oh! oh! I shall be caught! I shall be eaten!' And he began to run this way and that, searching for the hole in the hedge so that he could escape. He couldn't find it at all and he ran up and down the hedge, shouting 'Oh! oh! oh!' all the time.

The man with the beard was now stretching out his hands for the gingerbread man and it seemed he must surely catch him. But at the very last moment the little gingerbread man jumped. Up, up, and over the fishpond. SPLASH!! The man with the beard fell right in amongst the fish.

The gingerbread man felt very shaken. He had nearly been caught and he had nearly been soaked by the splash from the pond. And his hands were still very sore.

'Goodbye, Hedgehog,' said the gingerbread man to the round ball of prickles. 'I don't think I should have come with you after all.'

To his surprise, the hedgehog's head poked a little way out of the ball. 'Got your bread and milk, didn't you? Seems to me a chap like you doesn't know when he's well off.' And the hedgehog ducked back into his ball.

Slowly and not very carefully, the little gingerbread man crept through the hole in the hedge. He felt rather lonely because the hedgehog wasn't really his friend and he felt rather sad because he didn't seem to have been brave or clever that day. His song was so quiet even the gingerbread man himself hardly heard it.

'I'm not very happy, in fact I'm quite sad,
For I went with a hedgehog and didn't feel glad,
My hands are all prickled, I nearly got wet,
I'm the saddest that Gingerbread Man has been yet!'

And he only managed one little skip while he was singing.

13

The Gingerbread Man
Cheers Up

The next day the gingerbread man didn't feel quite so miserable. The sun was shining and his hands didn't hurt nearly as much as they had the night before. He saw the crow sitting in a dead tree being told off by his wife, and the gingerbread man laughed to himself and wondered what he should do on a nice sunny day with the fox in bed and the crow being scolded.

'The garden wasn't such a bad place,' he said to himself. 'I wonder if there might be some more bread and milk there? This time I shall be very careful indeed.' And the little gingerbread man ran across the fields and meadows until he came to the hedge around the garden.

He crept through the hole in the hedge as softly as thistledown, peering this way and that to make sure no one saw him. No one was there. All he could see was the blue bowl and a great muddy patch where all the pond water had made a mess of the lawn.

The gingerbread man laughed. 'That is what happens when people try and catch a gingerbread man!' he said. And when he looked in the bowl he found it was full of bread and milk, tasting even nicer than it had the night before, when the hedgehog ate most of it. The gingerbread man gobbled it up greedily and afterwards gave a happy sigh.

'I am feeling very much better,' he said to himself. 'I think I rather like this garden.' And he began to run and jump amongst the flowerbeds. He sat on the stem of a flag iris and slid right down to the bottom, and he laughed aloud in glee.

'That looks fun, little gingerbread man,' said a twittering voice. The gingerbread man looked up to see a swallow sitting on a wire above the roses.

'It is fun,' said the gingerbread man. 'Come and try it, Swallow.'

But the swallow twittered and flew into the air, dipping and soaring about the garden. 'I'm too busy for games. I have to go on a long, long journey and I must gather food to eat. When I have eaten all that I can, I must leave here and go somewhere warm. There's no time to play.' And he darted through the air, snapping up flies and insects.

The gingerbread man looked sadly after him, for he would have liked someone to play with. He went and stood on the stones at the edge of the pool and talked to the fish for a while.

'Hello little gingerbread man,' they whispered. 'We saw what you did yesterday. You must be careful.'

'I'm watching very carefully today,' said the gingerbread man. 'But I should like someone to play with me. Won't one of you come out and play?'

'We cannot leave our pond,' whispered the fish, and darted this way and that amidst the waterweed. The gingerbread man sighed and sang a little song:

'This garden is pretty and gives me such fun,
But I haven't a friend here, not even just one.
I wish there was someone who'd like to play,
And slide down the flowers in a gingerbread
    way.'

Just then he heard a buzz-buzz-buzzing from the flowers. He dashed across, and pushed his gingerbread nose deep into a bright red flower. There in the midst of it was a bee, drinking the nectar and carrying bags of pollen on her legs.

'Hello, Bee,' said the gingerbread man. 'Are you too busy to play?'

The bee looked up at him. 'I'm not supposed to,' she said shyly. 'I'm supposed to work all the day, bringing pollen and nectar to the hive. But I would like to play for a little while.' She put down her pollen and said excitedly, 'What shall we play?'

'We will chase each other through the garden,' said the gingerbread man and at once dashed away amongst the green leaves and the heavy-headed roses. The bee buzzed after him, laughing to herself as she flew.

The gingerbread man and the bee played and played and played. First the bee chased the gingerbread man until she landed on his nose, then he chased the bee until he caught her in his cupped gingerbread hands. At last, very tired indeed, they rested by the pond. All the little fishes whispered 'That looked fun.' And the gingerbread man said, 'It was very good fun indeed. Let's play something else.'

But the bee had been idle too long. Already she was gathering up her loads of pollen and hurrying about.

'Where are you going?' asked the ginger-bread man.

'They are waiting at the hive,' said the bee, buzzing anxiously. 'I have been away far too long. The grubs will be hungry, the honey won't be made, and the queen will be angry with me. I must hurry, hurry, hurry.'

'You are very busy,' said the gingerbread man.

'All bees are busy,' buzzed the bee. 'Look at

the time! I should never have stopped to play.'
And she flew into the air, her heavy pollen bags
weighing her down.

'Wait!' cried the gingerbread man. 'Can I
come and see your queen?'

'If you wish, if you wish,' buzzed the bee. 'But
I must hurry. Hurry!'

And she buzzed off out of the garden, with the
gingerbread man running very fast to keep up.
As he ran he sang a song:

'The garden today didn't scare me at all,
The bee and I played by the pond and the
  wall.
And now she must fly to the hive by the tree,
And Gingerbread's with her to see what's to
  see!'

And away he dashed, to meet a bee queen in a
bee hive.

14

The Gingerbread Man
Visits the Hive

As the bee buzzed busily over the fields, the gingerbread man ran after her, skipping and jumping all the way. The crow, sitting in a tree, saw him running.

'Where are you going, little gingerbread man? Why are you always running and jumping like that? Makes a body tired just watching you,' said the crow in his harsh, rough voice.

'I am going with my friend the bee to visit the hive,' said the gingerbread man. 'And I shan't stay and talk to you, bad Crow.' The gingerbread man dashed away across the grass. The crow flapped his ragged wings and rose in the air after him.

'Caark! Caark! You don't want to visit no hive. You want to come see a crow's nest, you do. Come with me, little man, come with me!' And the crow stretched out his dirty yellow claws to grab the little gingerbread man.

'Oh! Oh! Oh!' cried the gingerbread man, running even faster.

Suddenly the crow gave a startled 'Caark!' and

bounced up in the air. 'Get away from me, Bee, get away! I don't want to be stung, get away!' screeched the crow, for the little bee was buzzing angrily round him and the crow was frightened.

'I'll teach you, I'll teach you,' said the bee in her soft buzzy voice and with a last 'Caark!' the crow flapped quickly away back to his tree. 'What is the world coming to?' he muttered to himself as he combed his dirty feathers. 'Setting bees on a body. What next?'

The gingerbread man and the bee went on their way together. 'Thank you, Bee,' said the gingerbread man. 'I see you are a true friend.'

The bee giggled shyly and said, 'How nice you are, gingerbread man. But we must hurry back to the hive.' So they buzzed and dashed quickly over the meadow, beyond the stream, to the hive nestling by the hedge.

The hive looked just like a tall wooden box, but at the bottom was a slit and bees were flying in and out, in and out, all the time. Two big strong bees were guarding the entrance and as the friendly bee flew in they said, 'You're late, Griselda! What have you been doing?'

'I was helping the gingerbread man,' she said, and the sentry bees turned and stared fiercely at the gingerbread man, who was standing shyly by the hedge.

'Please may I visit the hive?' asked the ginger-bread man politely. 'I should so like to see your bee queen and all the little baby bees.'

The sentries whispered to each other. Then one turned and said, 'Very well, Gingerbread Man. But don't steal our honey!'

'I won't take anything!' said the gingerbread man, and quickly squeezed through the narrow opening and into the hive.

It was very dark inside, dark and sticky. Everywhere bees were buzzing busily, rushing here and there with loads of pollen and honey. The gingerbread man looked all about him, at the golden combs of sweet honey, and the little wax cells where the baby bees lived. Some honey got on his hand and he licked it. 'Mmmm!' he said, and then remembered that he wasn't to touch the honey. Fortunately no one had seen him.

Suddenly all the bees began rushing about even more busily. 'Her Majesty! Her Majesty!' they said one to the other, and stood respectfully to the side. The gingerbread man tried to squeeze out of the way too but it was very crowded and his gingerbread legs wouldn't squash up small. And the queen was coming, the bee queen with all her court.

When he saw her, the gingerbread man gasped. She was very tall and very slender, with a beautiful

furry coat and a golden crown on her head, which was so fine and delicate that it might have been made out of strands of honey.

'What a lovely bee!' he said breathlessly, and the queen heard him and turned.

'Who are you?' she asked in her high, buzzy voice.

'I'm the gingerbread man, Your Majesty,' said the gingerbread man, bowing low. 'I am visiting the hive.'

'You are welcome, little gingerbread man,' said the queen and waved one slender leg. 'Remember, you must not eat our honey.' She walked away, and all the bees in her court rushed around her, smoothing her path and combing her with their legs.

After that, the gingerbread man didn't know what to do. He wandered round the hive, where all the bees seemed to be working terribly hard. Then he found some big fat bees, lying on the ground eating honey. They had lots and lots of it, golden pools of lovely sticky honey.

'Hello,' said the gingerbread man.

'Hello, little gingerbread man,' said one of the bees, lazily munching. 'Have some honey.'

'I don't know if I should,' said the gingerbread man. 'I didn't think we were supposed to eat the honey.'

'We can do anything we like,' said the fat bee. 'We are the queen's husbands. We're the drones.'

'Well if you say I can perhaps I can,' said the gingerbread man and he sat down with the drones and began to eat the lovely honey.

He was soon very sticky. 'I like this hive,' he said happily. Just then his friend the bee came in.

'What are you doing, Gingerbread Man?' she

cried. 'You mustn't eat the honey!'

'Don't make such a fuss, Griselda,' said the drone, lying back half asleep. 'We like eating honey.'

But Griselda took the gingerbread man by the arm and rushed him away.

As he went all the bees saw how sticky he was and began to buzz. 'He's been eating honey, honey, honey. He's been eating honey,' they whispered, and from far away the queen's high voice sounded loudly. 'WHO's been eating honey?' she demanded.

'But they said I could,' said the gingerbread man.

'You must never, never listen to what the drones say,' said Griselda, and she and the gingerbread man went quickly to the door of the hive.

'Goodbye, little gingerbread man,' called Griselda.

'Goodbye, kind bee. I'm sorry I ate the honey,' said the gingerbread man.

'Perhaps we shall meet in the fields now and then.' And Griselda waved until the gingerbread man was out of sight.

He didn't run or jump very much because he was so full of honey. So he sang a little song instead:

'I went in the hive and I met the great queen,
The most beautiful bee that ever was seen,
But I gobbled the honey and shouldn't have
   done,
And now I am back in the warmth of the
   sun.

'I really shouldn't like to live in a bee hive,' said
the gingerbread man to himself, and gave a little
skip, the best he could do with his tummy so
full.

15

The Gingerbread Man
Has a Ride

In the morning, the gingerbread man woke up feeling very adventurous, and even braver than usual. His song showed how brave he felt:

'I'm a gingerbread man, as brave as can be,
There never was anything braver than me,
I run very fast, I haven't a care,
I'll even fly bravely right up in the air!'

And he turned a cartwheel to show that he meant it.

'Would you really, little gingerbread man?' said a twittering voice. 'Would you really be brave enough to fly in the air?' It was the swallow, fluttering around and watching him.

'Oh yes,' said the gingerbread man. 'I'm brave enough for anything.'

'Jump on my back then, little man,' said the swallow, swooping low. 'I am stretching my wings ready for my journey, and I will take you for a ride.'

Suddenly the gingerbread man wondered if he was really as brave as he thought. Flying might be dangerous, and if he fell his gingerbread self would break into crumbs! 'I'm too heavy for you, Swallow,' he said and sat down on a stone. 'Thank you but it wouldn't be fair.'

'Too heavy? A little man like you? Jump on my back, Gingerbread, we'll have such fun.' And the swallow swooped low again, waiting for the gingerbread man to jump on. So the little gingerbread man did!

Up, up, up they soared, with the gingerbread man holding tight to the swallow's feathers. How he wished he hadn't said he was brave! The ground seemed a very long way away, the trees didn't look big any more but as small as bushes. As they rushed through the air, the gingerbread man saw great fluffy clouds close by, and then they flew quickly right into one of them.

'It's all misty in here,' said the gingerbread man. 'And it's damp. Fly out, Swallow, or I shall go soggy.'

So the swallow flew out of the cloud into the sunshine once again. The gingerbread man began to enjoy himself very, very much.

'Faster, Swallow, faster!' he cried, and the swallow dipped and swooped, making the gingerbread man laugh with glee.

Suddenly as they swooped near the ground a big black bird rose up and flew near them. It was the crow.

'What you doing, Swallow?' he asked rudely. 'That's my gingerbread man, that's my supper.' He flapped his dirty wings.

'Go away, Crow,' twittered the swallow. 'I'm giving the gingerbread man a ride.'

'We'll see about that,' said the crow, and the gingerbread man clung tight to the swallow as the crow tried to grab him from the swallow's back. But he needn't have worried. The swallow quickly soared up into the air, far faster and far higher than the crow could go.

'Come back, come back!' screeched the crow, trying to flap faster. 'That's my gingerbread that is!' But he couldn't catch up, and at last he went to sit in his tree, very tired and very hot. 'Blast that gingerbread man,' he said to himself.

The gingerbread man and the swallow laughed. 'This is the best fun I have ever had,' said the gingerbread man and the swallow said, 'Being a swallow is much better than being a gingerbread man.' 'Oh no,' said the gingerbread man. 'I like being a gingerbread man, I like it very much.'

Just then he noticed a great many birds swooping and soaring in the air. The swallow saw them too and flew at once to join them. They were all swallows.

'Come, come, it is time to go,' twittered the swallows to each other. 'No time to lose. Winter is coming and we must go on our journey to Africa. Africa. Africa!' And they flew round and round while more and more swallows flew to join them. The gingerbread man's swallow flew too, so fast round and round that the gingerbread man had to close his currant eyes against the wind. 'Africa, Africa, Africa!' said the swallow in his twittering way.

'I don't want to go to Africa,' said the gingerbread man, and the swallow twittered, 'Must go! No time to lose!'

'But I must get off. Put me down on the ground, Swallow, don't forget me,' said the gingerbread man worriedly, because all the swallows were gathered now and at any moment they would set off on their journey.

'I must be quick,' twittered the swallow, and flying faster than ever he swooped down, down, down to the ground. 'Jump, Gingerbread Man, jump!' he called. And, frightened though he was because they were still a very long way up, the gingerbread man jumped.

'Ooooooooooohhhhhhhhh!' he cried as he fell down, down, down through the air. FLUMP! The gingerbread man landed right in the middle of a nice soft haystack.

'Goodbye, kind Swallow,' he called as he climbed down, with bits of hay all over him. 'Have a good journey.'

'Goodbye, little Gingerbread Man,' called the
swallow. 'We must go, for winter is coming. We
must go to Africa!' And off the swallows flew,
each little bird whispering 'Africa!'

'I wonder what winter is?' said the gingerbread
man to himself, feeling rather tired after his
exciting day. He snuggled down at the bottom of
the haystack, and sang a song about it.

'I flew with a swallow, I soared in the air,
This gingerbread man really hasn't a care.
But winter is coming, the swallows must go,
Though where they are off to I really don't
  know!'

And he snuggled down in the warm hay to
sleep.

16

The Gingerbread Man
in the Autumn

When the gingerbread man woke up the next morning and got out of his nice warm haystack he found that the sun wasn't shining.

'The sky is all grey,' he said crossly. 'And the leaves are turning brown and falling off the trees. Why are you falling off, Leaves? I like you much better when you're stuck on your branches.'

The leaves rustled in the wind and said in their rustling voices, 'We have to fall off, little Gingerbread Man. It is autumn now, and leaves always fall off in the autumn. The wind and the rain are coming, and soon it will snow!'

'Autumn, winter, what is everyone talking about?' said the gingerbread man crossly. And because he was rather cold he went running and jumping across the grass.

But the grass was strange that day too. It was stiff, with white stuff on it. 'What's the matter with everything today?' said the gingerbread man, rubbing his gingerbread toes, for the white stuff on the grass was making them very cold.

'It is autumn, little Gingerbread Man,' said a

low slow voice. 'There is frost on the grass and clouds in the sky. The wind is blowing cold and hard across the fields and meadows.' It was the snail, peeping out of his nice warm house.

The gingerbread man sat down to talk to him, hugging his gingerbread hands under his arms to keep them warm. 'What is autumn, snail?' he asked. 'What is winter? I don't like it when the sun doesn't shine and the swallows fly away. I don't like my gingerbread to get cold and damp.'

'It's the way of things,' said the snail sadly. 'After summer comes the autumn, and then the cold, cold winter. Look, all the animals are getting ready, they are gathering food and finding somewhere warm to sleep. That is what you must do, little gingerbread man. Hide away, little man, until the summer returns.'

So the little gingerbread man ran about all the day, looking for berries and nuts and anything else he liked to eat. Then he took them to the haystack and sat in the hay, all warm and cosy while the winds blew outside. But he didn't like it! There was nothing to do and no one to talk to. So the next day the gingerbread man went out again into the cold and he had to run and jump even faster to keep warm. He saw the harvest mouse, running about gathering corn.

'Hello, Mouse,' called the gingerbread man. 'I

see you are gathering food for winter. I've got a lot of food but I don't want to stay inside all the time. I shall run and jump through the field and the meadows just as I always have.'

The mouse looked very upset. 'You mustn't do that, little Gingerbread Man! The snow will come. The rain will fall on you. The wind will blow you to crumbs! Go and hide in the warm, Gingerbread Man, please!'

But the gingerbread man wouldn't. 'I'm not afraid of the winter,' he said bravely, and sang himself a song.

'Everyone here is gathering food
And I've gathered some too, like Gingerbread
    should,
But I'll not go and sleep all the winter away,
I'll run and I'll jump, through each winter
    day!'

And all through the autumn that is what the gingerbread man did, as the weather got colder and colder.

One morning when the gingerbread man woke up it was very cold indeed. When he went outside the wind was blowing so hard that every now and then a gingerbread crumb blew away and he had to run after it to fix it back on. And however much he ran and jumped he couldn't

get warm. The gingerbread man began to feel very sad.

'Caark! Caark! Now you see what a silly gingerbread man you are,' said a voice. It was the crow, sitting in a bare tree with his feathers all on end.

'You're as cold as I am,' said the gingerbread man miserably. 'What will you do in the winter, Crow?'

'Wait till it's over, of course,' said the crow. 'I hates winter, I does. But one of these days I'll eat a little gingerbread, that's what I'll do.'

And the gingerbread man felt so cold he thought perhaps the crow might eat him. He went on his way, shivering.

He was taking no notice at all of where he was going. The wind blew the leaves into piles round his feet and he trudged slowly through them. Suddenly he looked up. There, in front of him, was the fox.

'Hello, little Gingerbread Man,' she said, lazily combing her beautiful red whiskers. 'What do you think of my coat?'

The gingerbread man gazed at the fox in amazement. She had a coat more beautiful, thick and red than any he had ever seen. 'You are more beautiful than ever,' said the gingerbread man. 'I have never seen such a lovely coat.'

The fox laughed happily. 'I get a new one each

winter,' she said, smoothing it with an elegant paw. 'That's what you should do, little Gingerbread Man. Get yourself a coat if you want to be out and about in the winter. I shan't eat you today, you've been far too polite.' And off she went, very pleased with herself.

'I must get myself a coat!' said the gingerbread man. 'But where from?' Suddenly he thought of Mrs Rabbit. At once he began to run and jump again. He found her safe and warm in her burrow. 'Mrs Rabbit, Mrs Rabbit,' he called, 'can you spare some warm fur?'

Kind Mrs Rabbit came out of her burrow. 'What do you want it for?' she asked.

'I need to keep warm in the winter,' said the gingerbread man. 'If I don't have a coat I shall have to hide away all the time and I shouldn't like that at all.'

'That isn't the life for a gingerbread man,' agreed Mrs Rabbit. 'Let's see what I can do.'

The gingerbread man waited and waited. At last Mrs Rabbit put away her sewing needle and said, 'Try these for size, Gingerbread Man' and held out a jacket and a pair of woollen socks.

'Thank you, thank you, Mrs Rabbit,' called the gingerbread man, quickly putting them on. 'Now I am ready for winter.' He dashed away across the fields, running and jumping happily.

But his head still felt cold. 'I need a hat,' he thought, rubbing his gingerbread. Just then he ran under a tree, and there on the ground was the husk of a conker. It was in two halves, and one half had a nice thick stem. The gingerbread man picked it up and plonked it on his head. 'That's better,' he cried and ran on his way.

All day the wind blew and blew, but the gingerbread man wasn't cold. He ran and he jumped, enjoying himself just as much as he had in the summer. The crow watched from his cold tree and said crossly 'Blast that little gingerbread man! He's all warm and I'm too cold to catch him.'

And that night the gingerbread man settled down to sleep in his warm haystack, with his coat and his shoes and his hat by his side. 'I don't think winter's so bad after all,' he said happily. 'I'm sure I shall have lots of winter adventures too.' And as the wind blew and the rain hissed down, the gingerbread man slept quite comfortably and dreamed his gingerbread dreams.

Gingerbread Man Recipe

Makes 18–20 gingerbread men.

You will need:

200 g plain flour
75 g soft brown sugar
75 g butter
2 tablespoons golden syrup
1 level teaspoon baking powder
2 level teaspoons ground ginger
½ level teaspoon bicarbonate of soda

Method

Sift the flour, baking powder, ginger and bicarbonate of soda into a large mixing bow.

Melt the butter, sugar and syrup in a saucepan over a low heat. Do not allow the mixture to get hot.

Pour the melted mixture into the mixing bowl and stir into the dry ingredients with a wooden spoon, until you have a dough.

When the dough has cooled a little, turn it out on to a floured board and knead for a few minutes. Then roll the dough out to a thickness of about ½ cm. With a gingerbread man cutter, stamp out as many gingerbread men as you can.

You can then give your gingerbread men eyes and buttons using the currants.

Bake in a preheated oven at 200°C or Gas Mark 6 for about 10–15 minutes, or until the gingerbread men are slightly brown around the edges.

Allow the gingerbread men to cool for about five minutes before lifting them off carefully, and placing on a wire rack. When they are completely cold and firm, store in an airtight tin.